MY SCHOOL UNICORN

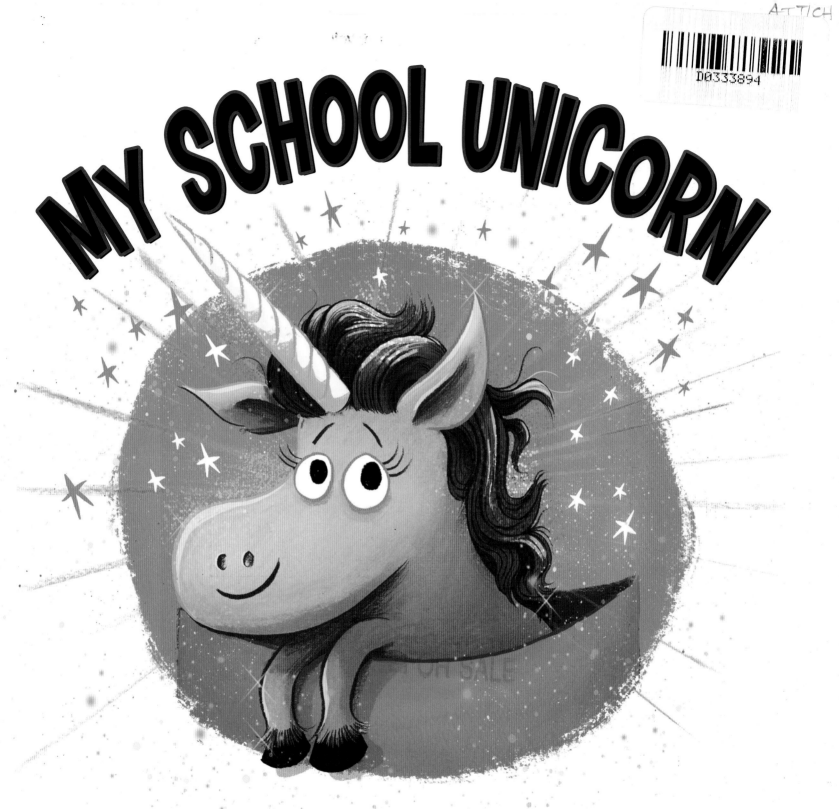

WILLOW EVANS AND **TOM KNIGHT**

For Lorelei Elizabeth Dewdney. Welcome to the world! - T.K.

HODDER CHILDREN'S BOOKS
First published in Great Britain in 2020 by Hodder and Stoughton

© Hachette Children's Group, 2020
Illustrations by Tom Knight

A CIP catalogue record for this book is available from the British Library.

ISBN 978 1 44495 642 9

1 3 5 7 9 10 8 6 4 2

Printed and bound in China

FSC
MIX
Paper from
responsible sources
www.fsc.org   FSC® C104740

Hodder Children's Books
An imprint of Hachette Children's Group. Part of Hodder and Stoughton
Carmelite House, 50 Victoria Embankment, London, EC4Y 0DZ

An Hachette UK company
www.hachette.co.uk
www.hachettechildrens.co.uk

Special thanks to Laura Roberts.

Hodder
Children's
Books

MY SCHOOL UNICORN

Willow Evans

Tom Knight

Evie loved story time with Dad.

It was the very best part of the day.

One night, as Dad tucked Evie in, he said, "Tomorrow is a special day. We're going to pick out your uniform for big school!"

Thinking about big school made Evie feel all **wobbly**.
Nursery was lots of fun, but school sounded scary.

Evie wished that things didn't have to change.

The next day, Evie's wobbly feeling hadn't gone away.
On the bus to the shops, her worries **grew** and **grew.**

"What if I don't make any
friends at big school?

BAG
FOR
BOOKS

"Look, Evie, we're here!" cried Dad.

Madam Lexi's Uniform Emporium was brimming from floor to ceiling with **clothes** and **shoes** in every colour for every occasion.

SCHOOL

FOOTBALL

BALLET

KARATE

"Welcome, Evie," smiled Madam Lexi.
"Would you like to try on your new school uniform?"

The uniform fit perfectly, but Evie still felt **wobbly.**

"Starting big school
is a **BIG** adventure,"
whispered Madam Lexi.
"This school unicorn might
be just what you need."

"Don't you mean school *uniform?*"
said Evie. Madam Lexi just winked.

Suddenly, Evie's pocket began to **wriggle** and **jiggle**, and . . .

PING!

Out popped a **teeny-tiny unicorn.** His mane sparkled and his pointy horn shone with a **shimmering** gold light.

"This is Bobby, your school unicorn," whispered
Madam Lexi. "Whenever you're worried,
he'll be there to help you feel brave."

"**Wow!**" gasped Evie. Bobby hopped up onto her
shoulder and nuzzled her cheek. The funny,
wobbly feeling began to fade away . . .

That afternoon, Bobby helped Evie get everything ready for her first day at school.

At bedtime, he curled up on a cushion beside Evie's bed. The **shimmering light** from his horn filled the room with a **happy glow.**

The next day, Evie and Dad
walked to **big school.**

Standing nervously outside the classroom, Evie put her hand in her pocket and felt Bobby give her a **reassuring nuzzle**. Knowing Bobby was there made Evie feel **brave** enough to pick up her bag and wave goodbye to Dad.

The classroom was
full of **new faces**.

Evie felt the **wobbly** feeling coming back.
But then Bobby hopped up onto her shoulder.
Evie took a deep breath and picked out an empty chair.

"Hello, I'm Evie," she said.
"Can I sit with you?"

"Yes!" Dylan and Zelda smiled back.

Evie spent the rest of the day with her new friends.

With Bobby by her side, new things didn't feel so scary, and her favourite things seemed even better.

Story time was **magical...**

CASTLES

music time was **funny...**

playtime was **exciting** . . .

and lunchtime was **yummy!**

The day flew by, and soon it was time to go home. Evie couldn't wait to tell Dad how fun school had been.

Evie and Bobby went to school together the next day and the day after that. Soon a whole week had passed, and Evie's wobbly feeling had **completely disappeared.**

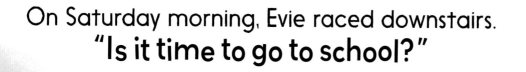

On Saturday morning, Evie raced downstairs.
"Is it time to go to school?"

"No, Evie," laughed Dad.
"Today's Saturday. There's no school today!"

"**Oh!**" Evie had been looking forward to seeing her friends.

"Don't worry, there'll be school on Monday," smiled Dad. "Now, why don't we go to the café for a special treat?"

"**Yes please!**" cried Evie.

On their way to the café, Dad and
Evie walked past a familiar shop.
Suddenly, Evie knew what to do.

"Wait there, Dad! I'll only be a minute!"

Dashing into the **Uniform Emporium,** Evie found Madam Lexi arranging the ballet shoes.

DING!

OPEN

"How nice to see you, Evie!
I thought you might be back."

Evie took a deep breath. "I think it's time for Bobby to help someone else. I don't feel scared anymore."

Madam Lexi smiled a **great big, twinkly smile.** Evie felt all warm inside.

Bobby hopped up on to Evie's shoulder and nuzzled her cheek. Then, with a swish of his tail, he jumped into Madam Lexi's pocket.

Evie smiled. "You were right, Madam Lexi. **Big school is a BIG adventure!**"